Walter Parke

The Skull Hunters!

A terrific Tale of the Prairie

Walter Parke

The Skull Hunters!
A terrific Tale of the Prairie

ISBN/EAN: 9783743331990

Manufactured in Europe, USA, Canada, Australia, Japa

Cover: Foto ©Andreas Hilbeck / pixelio.de

Manufactured and distributed by brebook publishing software
(www.brebook.com)

Walter Parke

The Skull Hunters!

THE
SKULL HUNTERS!

A

𝔗errific 𝔗ale of the 𝔓rairie!!

BY

CAPTAIN RAYNE MEADE,

AUTHOR OF

"THE PRAIRIE PUMPKIN," "THE INDIAN THIEF," "THE 'POSSUM CHIEF," "THE
KITCHEN RANGERS," "THE MOUSE TRAPPERS," "THE WARWHOOP OF
THE OJABBERAWAYS," "THE HUMBUG OF THE ROCKY MOUNTAINS,"
"THE MOSQUITO HUNTERS," "THE FLEA HUNTERS,"
"THE HOLMAN HUNTERS,"
ETC. ETC. ETC.

WITH NUMEROUS ILLUSTRATIONS.

LONDON:
JUDY'S PUBLISHING OFFICE, 73, FLEET STREET.

1868.

CONTENTS.

CHAPTER VIII.

CHAPTER IX.

CHAPTER X.

CHAPTER XI.

CHAPTER XII.

CHAPTER XIII.

CHAPTER XIV.

CHAPTER XV.

CHAPTER XVI.

CHAPTER XVII.

CHAPTER XVIII.

CHAPTER XIX.

CHAPTER XX.

CHAPTER XXI.

THE SKULL HUNTERS.

CHAPTER I.

A PRAIRIE RIDE.

AND of Anahuac! Region of Montezuma! How often on my Brazilian barb have I bounded over thy boundless snow - capped prairies and grass - grown mountains, in pursuit of 'possums, hyænas, boa - constrictors, and polar bears! How often have I been gored by buffaloes, kicked by 'coons, and chawed up by wild cats, in thy magnificent territory! How often have I partook of gin-sling, pumpkin pie, and brandy-cocktail, in the splendid locations that abound in thy vast dominion! Sweet land of Mexico! Glorious realm of Montezuma! Land of bowie-knives, skull-hunting, and plunder. Shall I ever forget thee? Not if I know it!

*   *   *   *   *

One day (ah! it is long, long ago!) I was mounted, as usual, on my matchless steed, bounding over the vast expanse of the prairie, which was now gleaming in the brilliant setting sun that heralded the approach of dawn. Far in the distance was seen the mighty range of the Sierra de Needella, or Needle Mountains, whose sharp points pierced the sky till it looked like perforated zinc. All was gay, bright, and serene. Wolves were howling, panthers growling, boa-constrictors hissing, and all other delightful sounds that could be imagined greeted the listening ear, in a sweet and soothing harmony.

I was attired in the usual costume of a Mexican hunter. My legs were encased in mocassins made of the skin of the laughing-jackass, which material, however, is naturally rather

inclined to *split*. Round my waist was a lasso
about two hundred feet long, in which was stuck
no end of bowie-knives, pistols, and other offen-
sive weapons. I was tattooed all up my back
in fast colours on an entirely new pattern, just
invented by that ingenious tribe the Squatchet-
maguzi Indians; while to complete my equip-
ment, my unrivalled rifle, which could carry
any distance in creation, was slung behind
me.

Thus equipped, I had ridden for hours, clearing the prairie of wild beasts as I went along,
and feeling within me that delight and ecstasy
which is only known to those whose lives are
passed in a continual state of danger and excitement.

Suddenly a dark figure, a tremendous distance
off, loomed before me.

"Who's that?" I asked myself. "Whoever
he is he must die!" and with that I raised my
telescope (thirty miles' range) in one hand, and
my revolver in the other, as is customary with
us hunters when firing, and pointed them
towards the figure.

"Jee-hosophat!" I exclaimed as I dropped
the pistol and telescope like a couple of red-hot
icicles, "it's a woman! I can see her as well as

possible, and can plainly distinguish the maker's name on her crinoline—THOMSON'S PATENT."

At this discovery I rode on still faster, until I arrived within about half a mile of the figure, when a voice which I should probably have recognized had I ever heard it before, cried out,—

"Oh, don't kill me, please, I am a woman!"

This exclamation startled me with its truth and loudness.

"So I perceive, fair señora," I answered, "and do not fear me, for I make it a rule never to kill any one unless there is something to be gained by it."

As I approached her I could perceive through her dark and thick mantilla (or rather woman-tilla) that she possessed the usual amount of beauty which falls to the lot of all Spanish ladies born in Mexico, or elsewhere.

"My name," she observed, in reply to an observation which I was about to make, "is Isabella Maria Elvira Serafina Inez de Fandango, daughter of Don Fernando Carlos Juan Bartolomeo Esteban Pomposo de Fandango, governor of Santa Vera Compostella Paz de Puebla. I am on my way to New Orleans to purchase a new dress, and shall be very glad of your company and protection on my journey through this vast and dangerous prairie."

To leap off my horse, kneel before her, kiss her hand, and express to her the solemn promise of my protection, and then to regain the back of my flying steed, was but the work of a second.

I was just about to commence a conversation of an interesting character, when I was inter-rupted by a warm current of air behind my back, and on looking round, saw my worst anticipations confirmed.

The prairie was on fire ! !

And not only this, but tremendous herds of wild beasts, driven by the flames, were rushing towards us !

"Onward, onward, quick ! " I exclaimed to the lady, "or we shall both be everlastingly obliterated ! "

Motionless with terror, she rode on as quickly as possible, while I followed at a still faster pace.

But we had scarcely galloped a few inches, when, on looking towards the east, a frightful yell, like that of a million of infuriated baboons, greeted my ears. I knew it but too well. It was the war-cry of the Prawnee Indians.

They appeared at the horizon; they were rushing towards us. Their name was Legion!

"Jee-roosalem!" I exclaimed, "this is indeed unlucky! These savages are on our trail. However, we shall easily be able to get away from them, if"—here I turned my eyes towards the opposite direction, and saw—oh, horror! ANOTHER host of yelling savages making their way towards us. I knew at a glance that they were that bloodthirsty and ferocious tribe, the Sawnees. They, too, to the number of thousands on thousands, were on our trail.

A PRETTY PREDICAMENT ON THE PRAIRIE.

CHAPTER II.

THE INDIANS.

I HAD incurred the resentment of these hostile tribes in two different ways. Having stopped once for three months at the Prawnee wigwams, I bade them an affectionate farewell and departed, but had scarcely ridden a hundred miles, when I discovered, on looking into my tobacco-pouch, that I had taken by mistake half a quarter of an ounce of bird's-eye belonging to an aged chief. I did not think it worth while to ride back and return it; but the tribe never forgave me, nor desisted in their endeavours to accomplish my capture and punishment.

My cause of quarrel with the Sawnees was somewhat different. Having made a magnificent and original joke to a child of the tribe, aged three years, I became so irritated at his not being able to see it, that I told him I believed the Sawnees were so called on account of the narrowness of their mental capacities. He told all the tribe, and they vowed the most deadly vengeance. I fled for my life, and had as narrow an escape as ever was known. A shot grazed my head as I rode away, and I am thankful to say, got clear off. Some months had elapsed since these events, and I had almost forgotten about them, but when I saw the two tribes pursuing me from opposite directions, I knew at once how matters stood. They had both chosen this as their settling day to pay off old scores, and visit with condign punishment the unlucky individual who had offended them. I particularly did not want to fall into the hands of the Prawnees, who had a way of pickling their dead enemies, and selling them to the captains of English vessels for preserved beef, which was anything but agreeable.

Determined not to be taken alive, I urged on my steed to his quickest pace, and my companion did the same. On, on we went, so quickly that our horses' hind legs frequently rode over their front ones, but my impatience even outstripped them, and I frequently rode quicker than my steed, so that I found myself, saddle and all, on his neck, and was obliged to wait till he advanced, to get back in my proper position.

Miles and miles we flew like lightning, and in less than an hour we flattered ourselves that we were out of danger, when—horror of horrors!— we found that the sun had set the prairie on fire at the OTHER end, and another vast troop of wild animals were rushing towards us from the northward!

Thus, north, south, east, and west, we were hemmed in by the most pressing dangers. If we went on it would be at the cost of our lives; if we rode back we should be killed; to turn to the right would be certain death; to the left, inevitable destruction; while to stay where we were would be utter annihilation.

Under these trying circumstances, it is not to be wondered at that, though a hunter of many years' standing (or rather *riding*), and therefore well accustomed to danger, my heart sank within me on beholding our desperate situation, and, even while whispering encouraging words to the lady, I could not help saying to myself— "Washington Busterville, my buoy, I guess you're in a tarnation fix!"

Nearer and nearer came our enemies; each moment was precious; what should we do?

Donna Isabella's horse, on perceiving our terrible position, was so overcome by terror and

affliction, that unable any longer to contain himself, he fell down, as those noble animals some-
times will, and died on the spot. My steed, by
good chance, was a Brazilian, and of stronger
nerve, so he was able to stand his ground
firmly

"Jump up behind me, quick!" I exclaimed
to my companion, "it is your only chance of
life." She obeyed, almost before the words had
reached my lips.

Nearer and nearer! we could hear the roaring
of the fire and the wild animals, the yelling of
the Prawnees, and the howling of the Sawnees,
in one wild unison.

The foremost herd of buffaloes were approach-
ing at a furious pace: in a few seconds they
would be upon us.

Our position was fearful—hopeless; not the
faintest chance of escape, from any quarter,
could we discern. Resistance was unavailing.

We stopped short in dismay and terror, and,
in an agony of desperation, waited the approach
of our deadly foes and our own inevitable
doom.

On, on they came!

The suspense was terrible!!

One moment more would decide our fate!!!

CHAPTER III.

OUT OF THE DILEMMA.

EADER, place yourself in our position, and then only can you realize what it is to find yourself in a burning prairie surrounded by tribes of buffaloes, anxious to exhibit your gore by means of their own, and herds of Indians thirsting for your blood, and hungering for minute slices of your liver!

But my presence of mind (and body) were both equal to the occasion, and I had determined what to do. As soon, therefore, as the nearest herd of buffaloes had arrived within a measured yard of where we stood, I urged on my gallant steed, who, clearing the head of the foremost buffalo with one mighty bound, alighted nimbly on the backs of those beyond. Once there we were safe.

Before us stretched a boundless expanse of bounding buffaloes' backs, forming a plateau as flat as Tupper, and as compact as Carlyle. No turnpike road could be smoother, or more convenient, for, with the exception of occasionally stumbling over the elevated tails or humps of the infuriated animals, we made our way with the ease and celerity of greased lightning.

Now, dearest reader, if you know of any neater dodge to get out of such difficulty as that I have just described, I'll trouble you to mention it. But I'm sure you don't—it's impossible. I've written two hundred and fifty tales of the prairie, and I ought to know. Rather!

My gallant barb behaved admirably. Though he was covered to the very hoofs with foam, though he was hamstrung with fatigue and spavined with terror, though his eyes flashed fire and filled with water, and though he panted to that extent that a pair of pants came from his nostrils at least every two seconds—still he urged on his wild career. He understood the slightest hint. I had only to dig my spurs into his ribs till they met in his inside, and the noble animal would immediately accelerate his pace in the most miraculous manner.

Onward, still onward, we pursued our way in a slantindicular nor'-nor'-easterly direction, dodging the prairie flames, and hoping by this policy to insure our lives from fire.

Hark! what is that fearful crash, similar to the breaking of a dozen banks, the thunder of six earthquakes, and the collision of forty express trains, all joined together? The living road beneath us quivers with the harrowing shock! It is—what?—

It is the fearful concussion of the two tribes of Indians and the two herds of buffaloes, meeting together in the middle of the prairie. They are at a complete dead-lock, and not all the police in the world could make them move on.

Listen! That wild combined yell is the concentrated essence of piled up agony!

I close my eyes with horror, and stop my ears with a couple of pistols—all is over!!!

*   *   *   *   *   *

The next day not a vestige remained either of the Sawnees, the Prawnees, or the buffaloes.

They had all closed together in a universal and indiscriminate slaughter, and mutually annihilated each other. Not a hair of a buffalo's tail, or a streak of an Indian's war-paint, was left to tell the tale of this fearful encounter. The prairie, too, had been afterwards completely destroyed by the fire, and what made it all the more shocking was, that it was totally uninsured!!

* * * * * *

So pass away all earthly things! So perish the black-beetles of Anahuac before the mighty glance of Harper Twelvetrees, and so sink the realms of Montezuma beneath the chawing-up majesty of the all-fired American Eagle!!

THE CAPTAIN AND BILL BOWIE FRATERNALLY EMBRACE.

CHAPTER IV

THE TRAPPER'S HUT.

THE sun had gone down with all hands, and Night had cast a veil of spotted *tulle* over the fair face of Nature, when we arrove safely at the end of our long and perilous journey.

Five hundred miles had we ridden that day over the backs of bounding buffaloes! And we felt tired!! Slightly!!!

Before us was a desirable opening in the forest, on which stood a hut utterly embosomed in trees, and built of the logs taken from various ships.

This lodge was built according to the strictest rules of logic, and through the open door we caught a glimpse of a beautifully carved table of logarithms.

Before the door stood a figure in a brown study and a bearskin suit of the same colour.

I knew him well; it was my old friend Bill Bowie, a back-(and front) woodsman, and a critter of the clearest imaginable grit.

On seeing us he started up as if struck by lightning.

"Thunder and blacking-brushes!" he exclaimed, "what do my eyes behold? Chaw me to pulp if it ain't the Captin!—his own festive self! Welcum, old hoss, welcum, to the very backbone of your toe-nails!"

"Bill," I cried, choking with emotion, "Bill, my own especial cuss, how art thou?"

And we rushed together in a most fraternal embrace.

Suddenly remembering Donna Isabella, I said, "Bill Bowie, yonder fair señora has ridden more than five hundred miles this blessed day, and she feels rather fatigued. Of course you have a drawing-room, a boudoir, two sleeping apartments, and four maid servants, all ready prepared for her reception?"

"Not much I ain't," returned the trapper, "but sich accommodation as my humble purse and my limited cot will afford, is yours till death. Come this way, and put yerselves outside whatever you can hold."

We responded joyfully to this cordial and spirited invitation.

"But my poor hoss," I suddenly exclaimed, "requires your hospitality. See, he reels from real fatigue, his walk is groggy, though he is evidently out of spirits, and his legs, which have hitherto made such extensive advances, brutally refuse to support him any longer." But our efforts were in vain. The noble and chivalric animal was half-drowned in his own foam, and could only draw his breath by means of pencils made especially for the purpose.

Accordingly, Bill Bowie and myself set to work, and built a stable over him where he lay, with all the latest improvements. In this stable, though rather an unstable resting-place, he passed the rest of the night. We entered the hut, and with a very good will quickly disposed of all Bill Bowie's (eatable) property, of course cutting off the hen-tail, but solacing ourselves with a cock-tail of brandy afterwards.

Over our grog, but, of course, under the influence of it, Bill Bowie began to relate some experiences of his hunter's life, in a manner which proved that, though a trapper, he by no means, in the matter of conversation, could be called a Trappist.

Alluding to the Brawnees, an exceedingly blood-thirsty and rum-thirsty tribe of Indians in the neighbouring forest, Bill related the following narrative :—

" They cum here a week or two ago," he said,

"rushing out of their own broad-wood to surround my humble cottage, and yelled their war-cry with such thunderacious louditude that they took the roof clean off the house, and shook every winder to powder, besides frightening every bit of flesh off my poor dog 'Caution,' who died that very night!"

Here the rough backwoodsman leant upon his rifle, and wiped away a tear with the butt-end.

"But this is weakness," he remarked tearfully, gazing into his glass of grog; "why should I give way to solemncoliness? While Bill Bowie can hit a humming-bird's right eye at three hundred and fifty yards, and take off an Indian's war-paint from the other side of the prairie, I calkilate he needn't be skeered—not much!"

At this instant a wild and unearthly yell greeted our ears with great cordiality.

"Jeeroosalem and pumkin squash!" cried the trapper, starting up and seizing his rifle. "It's them, captin, sure as cubs is licked!"

"Who?" I asked, breathlessly, as the wild yell was repeated in such a manner as to make all the colour rush from our faces into the soles of our boots.

Bill Bowie replied in a hissing whisper, that sounded really awful in the silence—"THE SKULL HUNTERS!!!"

CHAPTER V.

THE RAID OF THE REDSKINS.

IT is impossible for any pen but mine to describe the consternation excited by these fearful words!

Donna Isabella **turned** so pale **as to** be almost invisible, and would undoubtedly have fainted, had there been anything in the hut soft enough to fall upon,

which there wasn't.

The complexion of poor Bill became completely

bil-ious; his eyes started from his head as if on a long journey; his tongue clove to the soles of his feet; his limbs refused to perform their office —even at an increased salary, and every hair, not only of his head, but of his bear-skin suit, stood on end more persistently than the egg of Columbus.

As for myself, nothing but my own undaunted bravery prevented me from being extremely frightened, but, as it was, the only feelings I experienced were a knocking together of the teeth and the knees, and a peculiar sinking sensation at the pit of the stomach.

Had we not cause to fear? Were not the Skull Hunters the terrors of the prairie? Did not the very sound of their name frighten away the appetite of the ferocious jaguar, and send the prairie-snake into epileptic convulsions? Was not their chief, Wanderoga—surnamed the 'Coon-Licker—known to be a man who would stick at nothing but the throat of an enemy, and whose feverish thirst for blood not all the soda-water in the universe could allay? And, above all, they had the terrific custom of skull-hunting, about which the reader may perhaps be curious. It consists of taking prisoners, and cutting out their skulls by means of a circular kind of bowie-

knife made especially for the purpose. To do
this at a single stroke, without spilling one drop
of blood, and so dexterously that even the victim
himself does not feel it, is considered rather a
clever feat in that part of the world, and in this
feat the Brawnees, or Skull Hunters, particularly
excel. Of course it leaves the head of the victim
in rather a tender condition, and it is owing to
the prevalence of this custom that the natives of
Mexico are in general so remarkably soft-headed.

* * * * *

And these were the ferocious people who were
now coming down upon Bill Bowie and myself
like all vengeance, in order to trap the trapper,
and visit condign punishment on the man who
had caused the extinction of the Sawnees and
the Prawnees, their kindred tribes!!

* * * * *

The moment for action had now arrived. Bill
Bowie roused himself, and having loaded his
rifle with all the gunpowder in his tea-caddy,
together with a charge of grape from a packet
of grocery on the table, he stood boldly on the
defensive, while I stood cautiously on the table,
and looked out of window

In order to survey our enemies, I raised to

my eye the trusty telescope, a splendid instru-
ment of about forty-five horse-power, through
which the events of the ensuing week could be
clearly discerned. The action in the present case
was rather imprudent, for, while our enemies
were near enough in all conscience, the telescope
brought them considerably nearer.

" Great Powers of Jee-hosophat!" I exclaimed,
" it is indeed the Skull Hunters! See! they are
bowling their war-whoops, and letting fly their
toma-hawks!"

Bill agreed with me that these were bad signs.
On came the Indians. Foremost rode the ferocious chief, Wanderoga, mounted on a mighty
Moque, or Mexican Donkey. In stature he was
so tall as to reach the poll—of his own head.
In his hand he held a *Tomahawk*, which looked
capable of bestowing on the head of an enemy
such a *Punch* as few would be disposed to look
upon as *Fun*. As an emblem of his wisdom, in
his *Judy*-cial authority over his tribe, an *Owl*
was embroidered on his cloak, having no horns,
which showed that the artist had not considered
it necessary to *Horn-it*. The other horny-ments
of his costume consisted entirely of skulls, either
real, or carved by some Indian scul-ptor in the
most skull-ful manner.

A FIRE—AND NO ESCAPE.

The reader may perhaps wonder how I noticed all this, but the fact is, that the sun had just risen in the south-west, for the sole purpose of illuminating the exciting scene which was to follow.

"Mis-creant—or rather Mr. Creant—of a pale-face!" the terrific chief thundered, his eyes lightening with anger; "give me that 'bacca back a-gain, or the pipe of peace shall be for ever broken between us!"

"Hound of a white man!" cried another chief, "recall thy dog-grel jest against the Saw-nees, or thou shalt find it no joke!"

My answer to these questions was pointed—so was my gun—at the head of the chief. But, unfortunately, the rifle, like the Indians, refused to go off.

The Redskins surrounded the hut, and a fearful fight commenced between us. Though speedily disarmed, I fought with desperation, which was at that time the only thing I had to fight with. Bill defended the buil-ding with great a-bil-ity, but in vain. Poor Bill, he felt he was dishonoured, though he knew he would soon be taken up!

The Indians smashed all the windows, and set fire to the hut in ninety-two places. I then began to fear that we were gone 'coons to a slight extent.

Seizing an opportunity in one hand, and Donna Isabella in the other, I escaped to the roof, where a ruef-ul spectacle presented itself. All around us were fiery Indians, and all beneath us was the fiery habitation. I had long burned to distinguish myself in an engagement of this kind, but now I feared that I should burn till I could not be distinguished by any one else.

As for Bill, I regarded him as the gonest of 'coons. "Poor fellow," I murmured, "sad is thy fate, to be burnt in thy habitation, and to be burnt out at the same time!"

CHAPTER VI.

THE ESCAPE FROM THE HUT.

OU will protect me, Señor?" cried Donna Isabella.

"Fear not, Bella Señorita," I replied, "I will defend you with my own life," (meaning, of course, that I could defend my own life and her along with it.)

The flames increased every moment, and I saw plainly that unless they could be got under, all would be over.

"Fuel that I am to stay and be burnt!" I cried; "I will escape by hook or by crook— probably the latter. Ah, Señora, I see a chance of escape!"

At a short distance below stood a noble moque, tied to the thickly-spreading branches of an axle-tree, and munching the festive thistle.

Seizing my fair companion with a firm grasp, I gave one tremendous bound, and parting my legs as I fell, alighted safely on the moque's saddle, with my feet in the stirrups and Donna Isabella secured behind me. All I had to do was to cut the animal's bonds, and start off over the prairie. (N.B. This clever feat was entirely my own invention, and the patent has since been secured.)

Thus we were flying in hot haste from the burning hut.

Hurrah! *Vive la chasse!* Free once more! Onward we fly across the prairie, swift as the agile Léotard, or the magnificent Menken!!!

But the Indians were after us in something like seven-eighths of a jiffy (which is Mexican for a second).

The terrific chief Wanderoga unfurled his lasso and hurled it after us.

We had ridden three-quarters of a mile, but

the lasso was well aimed, and caught both of us, the steed included, in its folds.

We were now in the chief's power. He hauled in his lasso to the tune of " Tom Tough," and thus pulled us towards him. Consequently, we were obliged to proceed backwards in the most uncomfortable manner. We were soon in the very centre of the Indians, taken prisoners, and secured. The fierce Wanderoga recognized Donna Isabella.

" It is *her !*" he exclaimed ; " but stay,"—and here he referred to a beautiful pocket edition of Lindley Murray,—" I mean it is she ; Donna Isabella, light of my eyes, you are mine !"

" Oh, spare me, great chief !" she cried, " why do you thus persecute the daughter of the pale-faces ?"

" Because of my love for you," he replied, " which devours my entire soul, leaving me at the mercy of the nearest fishmonger, and because also of thy riches. Thou art a mine of wealth, and I," he proudly added, " am a minor."

" Great chief," cried the Donna, " methinks this is strange language to one who has never seen you before in her life ?"

" Perjured daughter of the pale-faces !" he thundered, " were we not acquainted for two minutes and a half nineteen years ago, when you were an infant in arms against your nurse's breast, and I was an Indian in arms against the government ?   No longer shall your false air deceive me.   You must leave the chignon of civilization for the wig-wam of the red-skins, and become the squaw of Wanderoga!"

"Never, never !" cried Donna Isabella, with a shriek that resounded throughout the prairie.

"I have said. My men, take this squaw—this squa-lling lady to the tents, which, to all in-tents and purposes, are my dominions."

His commands were obeyed long before they were spoken.

"As for this miscreant," he added, alluding to me, "who bears the (two-penny) stamp of guilt upon his brow, he must be taken to the post, though not on any account delivered, and his fate shall be sealed this very day."

Six Indians instantly started off to procure sealing-wax for this purpose. I felt my heart sink to twenty degrees below zero at these fearful words.

A WARM—NOT TO SAY HOT—RECEPTION BY THE INDIANS.

CHAPTER VII.

MY LIFE (AND DEATH) IS AT STAKE.

WHAT was to be my fate? Was I to die or be killed? Was I to be led away like a lamb to the scaf-fold? (O, lam-entable fate!) or would the Indians-take my life by means of the stake? —which would be anything but tender.

"Hold we, or let us hold, a council of judgment," cried the ferocious but grammatical Wanderoga, "and decide how this son of an insolvent skunk is to be helped out of his mangy existence. Squashereego woogo whang!" (This was the signal to assemble). The chief having thus piped all hands, and some attendants having handed all pipes to the assembled warriors, they formed a select circle on the grass, and commenced operations. Some were for suspending my punishment, and others for suspending me, but the majority moved for a division of me into little bits, in order to make me a man of parts. At length, however, it was decided, after a hot discussion, that I should undergo the ordeal of fire

"Let him be instantly bound," cried Wanderoga, "in three volumes of smoke, and as he has already been hot-pressed, he must now be lettered on the back. Then publish it to the world that I am the author of this work."

These literary commands were obeyed literarally. The stake was brought and fixed, and I could not help thinking that it appeared very well done.

"Now, tie him," said Wanderoga.

"Ty-rant," I cried, "hast thou no conscience?"

"Nary bit," answered the redskin. "I lost it all seventeen years ago, through a frightful attack of the measles, and by medical advice have been skull-hunting ever since for the benefit of my health. Go, my men," he added, "and bring from the other side of the river—sticks, and send him to the burning regions."

So I was bound, and raised to the exalted post of—ten feet high, and tied to it with a portentous—a Daven-portentous knot, a complete Gordian knot; indeed, as it was made of the brightest coloured ribbons, I may say that it was a very gaudy-'un. They piled up the sticks, and stuck up the pile immediately beneath me; then Wanderoga applied a paraffin match with all the malice of Lucifer himself, the flames rose and the Indians gave a yell of triumph, and appropriately shouted one of the songs of Burns.

That I should either die or live I felt assured, but I thought I had better become unconscious for a little while, and thus remove the necessity of a long description when I came to write a record of these adventures. But the fearful heat! oh, my stars!—

*   *   *   *   *

Bang! What is that terrific roar, like thunder seen through a magnifying glass?—I open my eyes!—Joy! joy! a rifle bullet has pierced the Gordian knot, gone clean through the post, and taken off the scalp of an Indian behind. My bonds slowly unloose—I am free once more. I gave one mighty leap from the post and alight on the prairie. The Indians have fled in terror. A figure rushes towards me with a shriek of ecstasy,—

"Captin!—Hail, Columbia!!—Likewise the star-spangled banner!!! Guess I've caterwaumpussed 'em, some! and thou, hoss of mine, art free!" and he waltzed with glee.

"Bill, my cherishedest chum!" I cried, "how escapedst thou?"

"Saw all was over; laid down, blew up the

hut with a pinch of powder, killed six Injens and sent myself high up, and slick on a gum-tree, safe as sarce; looked through yer spyer, saw yer danger, and tuk a real life aim; and the end justerfies the means!"

"Bill, thy valour is invalourable. But where, and oh, where, is my Isabella gone? Ah me! she is gone from my gaze; it may be for years, it may be for ever—but if she loves as I have loved, she never can forget!"

And I shed tears on a liberal scale.

CHAPTER VIII.

MORE ADVENTURES.

'RAPS, Captin, you'll soon find heragin," suggested the consoling Bill Bowie.

"Carrambo! If I don't," I sobbed, "I'll hang my harp on a willow-tree, and go where glory waits me, then let me like a soldier fall, on the banks of the blue Moselle! But if once again I find

my Donna Isabella—my Donnarest of Isabellas
—we will never, never part—not even our
hair !"

Having wept industriously for about an hour
and twenty minutes, I arose, feeling as perfectly
composed as many pieces by Gounod. Then
with my lasso I caught my bounding steed, who,
having been set loose by the Indians, had re-
lapsed into pristine wildness. Once more mounted
and in a splendid frame—of mind—I was commencing my pilgrimage, when Bill, looking up
at the nearest tree, exclaimed, " Snakes and sawdust, Captin, if thar ain't a b'ar just ready to
spring on to us ! look !"

" Let him be no bar to our progress, Bill," I
answered, " neither act barbarously towards him.
Though the bear is impatient, bear with him
patiently ! for he is evidently prepared to fight
for bear life !"

" Grizzly, thine hour of croaking has arrove !"
cried Bill, and with this he laid an artful trap for
the animal by placing immediately under the
tree a loaded pistol, which the bear no sooner
saw, than he endeavoured to possess himself of.
With a fierce growl, he leaped upon the weapon,
and in so doing, placed his paw on the trigger,

which went off and shot him through the exact centre of the heart, as Bill, with mathematical accuracy, had arranged.

"Bravo!" cried Bill, who then proceeded to skin the bear, for the purpose of bearing the skin away in triumph. He then boned all the bones, and took away as much of the flesh as he thought meet. I never saw a bear so miserable when alive, or so much cut up when dead.

The morn had now broken, making, of course, a stupendous whole in the sky It was a beautiful day, notwithstanding the fact that it rained and hailed, and snew, and thundered; that the lightning flashed, and the wind blew from every point in the compass, and several out of it; for these conflicting elements, all acting at the same time, so balanced and counteracted each other, that they restored Nature to her equilibrium, and rendered the weather perfectly moderate and delightful.

Once again we made tracks, and _O sangre de diez mil hipopotamos!_ how charming was that ride over the unlimited prairie, with the sweet consciousness that every blade of grass concealed a snake or a jaguar, and that the atmosphere was alive with the most appalling dangers!!

We had not proceeded far—rather under five

hundred miles than over—when we heard a hissing as of an enraged playgoer, and iss-uing from a neighbouring morass, we saw, as we anticipated, an enormous crocodalligator—one of those ferocious reptiles which are so plentiful both in the Great Dismal and the Little Cheerful Swamp. The monster was about sixty feet long, and of proportionate bulk. He charged at us with his tremendous jaws wide open, as if with the dishonest intention of taking us both in. A fearful conflict commenced between the reptile and Bill Bowie. As for myself, my courage is of so high an order, that I do not like using it except on special occasions, for fear of injuring its quality; so I rode at a safe distance, and exhorted Bill to be valorous.

Which he was. He tried the scales of the reptile, and found them quite true, though so hard that he could make no impression upon them, and he might have "fit and fit," till the end of all things, but that—

Heavens! can I believe my ear-sight? or is it "Yah, yah!" and "O golly!" that I hear issuing from the reptile's mouth? Yes, it is, it is! for the very next moment the crocodalligator suddenly burst with a loud explosion, and a nigger leaped out of his jaws. Immediately

QUANKO DISCOURSETH DULCET MELODY.

refreshing himself with a bath in the lake, the emancipated one approached us. Meanwhile the crocodalligator had died from exhaustion consequent on the sudden and unexpected vacuum in his inside.

"Cullered one," asked Bill, "how on airth came you in the interior of that ere gorgonious quadruped?"

"Golly, massa! I'll splain at wunst. My name is Quanko; I was reared on a ricery down in old Kentuck, till massa bust out about my drinking thirteen bottles of rum a day, which he said was a sight too much. So dis child cut, he did, and the slavers was arter him full pelt. I was hunted to this ere creek, where I jumped in and was swallowed whole directly by this scaly cuss. But it put the hunters off the scent, and I've been pooty snug, considering, the whole three days. But now I'm free, free, yah, yah! golly, whoo!!"

"But haven't you heard," I asked, "that the negroes are all set free in the United States, and the white men have been made slaves instead?"

"I ain't heard it, massa; but this I know, I'm a man, and a brudder, and have been so a considerable spell, yah, yah!"

" Quanko," I cried, " I feel for you—I dew—
so I'll tell you what—can you play and sing?"

The swarthy one drew a banjo from his
waistcoat pocket, and commenced the ravishing
strains of " Hoop-de-dooden-do!" in a manner
that brought tears to the green part of my left
eye.

" Heavenly!" I exclaimed. " So you be off
instanter to London, and take this note, with
my compliments, to the Manager of the Only
Original Christy Minstrels (who never perform
out of London), and tell him to bring you out
immediately, or dread the consequences. And
so, skedaddling son of Afric, fare thee well!!"

The man of colour took the recommendation
with two hips, accompanied by a hooray, and
disappeared. The next moment he was spinning
over the prairie at the usual speed of the negro,
the Derby, and other races, and we could hear
the dulcet strains of his banjo in the charming
melody,—

> " I'm goin', I'm goin', to see dat happy nation ;
> I'm goin', I'm goin', to leab de ole plantation!"

CHAPTER IX.

A TRAVELLING PARTY ON THE PRAIRIE.

UR negro-cia-
tions with
Quanko being
thus con-
cluded, and
that nigger
himself having
disappeared
over the edge
of the horizon
—we fervently
hoped, without
any injury —
we again made
tracks over
those parts of
the prairie which most required them.

We travelled on at a pace varying between
hat of a snail and a whirlwind, until we over-

took a party consisting of four persons, and though the number was complete, we could see that there was one short—the rest were rather tall than otherwise. As they were all dressed alike in sombreros, capas, and black masks, their appearance, though noble, was not distinguished —at least, we could not distinguish them very well, for we could only tell one from the other by comparing each with the rest, and separating the residue from the remainder. All were mounted on the finest Brazilian Arab steeds, covered with such trappings as only the most experienced trappers could produce. The chief of this peculiar party—who appeared rather a peculiar party himself—was evidently the leader, so we spurs on to this-person, and I asked him, in tones of almost grovelling politeness : " Who the blazes are you, and where on earth are you going ? " The stranger drew himself up and stood upon his dignity—which, of course, made him look much taller than before—and replied proudly, " Sir, I am Young."

"Young!" I exclaimed, "excuse me, but I thought you looked rather old. But ' appearances,' as the Greek poet Herod Antipater observes, ' is deceiving.' "

" Stranger, I am Brigham Young, though I

confess that I was once Brigham younger. Very much so."

"*Squashez de Pumpkino!*" I cried, "am I indeed speaking to that great man on whom the Stagg and Mantle of the prophet Smith has descended? O Jehillakin! Vouchsafe, great chief, to let me and my chum join your party, for the company of a high prophet is of course highly profitable."

"I am bound," remarked Brigham, "for the tents of the Brawnees, for the purpose of bringing home a fresh wife to the Salt Lake, after which I shall return to Utah, and should like you-ter go with me. Of course you have seen the Great City?"

"No," I answered, "I have not been to Drury Lane for some time, but—no matter—say, thou Mormonest one, what is the name of the lady who is destined to receive the next dividend of thy affections?"

The great prophet took out his morocco pocket-book and referred to it.

"Her name," he replied, "let me see—No. 467 Division 13. Her name is—er—er—Bella——"

"Is-a-bella!" I bellowed. Oh, could it be possible that my own one was destined to be taken away to the Mormons, than whom a more-mons-trous set of perverted Christians did not exist? The thought was madness!

"Oh, do not say," I implored, "that her name is Donna Isabella Maria Elvira Serafina Inez de Fandango!" (Here I stopped to take breath.)

"I ain't going to say so, stranger," replied the prophet, "but I calkilate it is."

"Oh, my prophetic soul!" I cried, "my uncle! (if I may use that familiarity) pray strike; but hear me. I love Donna Isabella with an affection that will outlast time, eternity, perpetual motion, the Reform Bill, and all sublunary things; I love her to an extent that has completely taken away my appetite, and made me go without food for three hours and a half. Grant me, therefore, the Donna, if I can find her—you surely cannot miss one missus out of 467 ; and I will give you all I hold dear, even half the profits of my next romance of the prairie, which is certain to go like steam!"

With a generosity I never saw equalled—far less excelled, the great prophet agreed to take fifty per cent. more than I offered. The bargain was struck on the spot, and Isabella's name was struck off the list. My heart bounded so as to lift me almost off my horse, and I gave a prolonged shriek of gratitude.

Our cavalcade proceeded till we reached the fork of the River Plate, where a most affecting scene took place. One of the party was about to take his departure, and, like most men, he seemed very unwilling to part with his prophet.

"Venerable and prophetic being," he cried, "my hour is come, and I must go. Farewell! and if sixteen pages of praise in the *Athenæum* can satisfy thee, thou shalt have it with all my heart."

They closed in a long and fervent embrace, mutually bathing each other in tears, and were almost pulled off their horses by the struggle. The scene was so affecting that we all wept in concert—keeping capital time—and our horses did the same. Every bird in the neighbouring trees sobbed with an inexpressible anguish, and even the grizzly buffalo and the catawampus panther were observed to wipe their eyes with their long and melancholy tails. In a few moments the stranger had skedaddled. Such is life.

"Who was that?" I asked the Prophet.

"His name," he replied, "is W. H-pw-rth

D-x-n, who came from Old England to visit New America. He has sojourned in the promised land for a considerable spell, and now departs in tears and Mexican mocassins. He will go home and write a book about the Salt Lake, which my prophetic power tells me will run to six editions. What troubles me is, that he wouldn't accept my offer of seventeen of my wives, which I chose from among the oldest, and consequently most worthy of respect, but when I made him the offer, he seemed slightly kerwollopped, and said he kinder reckoned he couldn't."

I now turned to the tall and short cavaliers, one of whom had a white coat under his capa, and a double-headed eagle on it ; and the other a dark complexion, and a head of hair whose like I shall not look upon again. Slapping them on the back with great respect, I cried, " Well, my hearties, and who are you ? "

They both replied simultaneously—particularly the shorter one—" My name is Max "— cried he.

" My name is Max "—cried the other.

Here they both stopped in a sudden fit of prudence. But their reticence was too late ; for so loudly had they spoken, that the echo, reverberating from the opposite side of the prairie, sent back the latter halves of the names about two seconds after they were spoken—

" ——imo ! "

" ——imilian ! "

At these words the scales fell from my eyes, and a sudden light shone upon me—so you may judge what a state my visual organs must have been in.

CHAPTER X.

THEIR IDENTITY DISCOVERED.

KNEW them both now, well. Grasping the hand of the taller one, I said, " I ain't much up in titles; but I kinder guess I'm real glad to see that your Royal Serene Highness of an all-fired Imperial Majesty——"

" Not that name," the cavalier answered, sternly; " I've had quite enough of it, thank you. As an arch-duke I can bridge over most difficulties; but, as an Emp-eror, I run some chance of a hemp-en rope. I am now plain Maximilian——"

"Not very plain, either," I remarked. (N.B. This was a compliment.)

"And, having had quite enough of the beauties of Mexico, I am now going to my Mar—to my Mira—mar." (Here, he was almost drowned in emotion.) "One legacy," he added, "I will leave to this unhappy country, and of that I must beg of you to take charge, and deliver it into the hands of any future governor of the country who may require it." He handed me a sealed packet, saying, "You will preserve this inviolate."

"Most decidedly," I answered, and immediately afterwards, in pure forgetfulness, I broke it open, and perused the contents.

It was a formal declaration of the reasons why the undersigned had retired from the government of Mexico, coupled with some words of warning and very sensible advice to all future rulers of the country Enclosed in it was a free pass to any respectable lunatic asylum for any one who should attempt to become Emperor of Mexico.

As we rode on, I turned my attention to the smaller cavalier, and said, "Well, Maximo, my hearty, how are you, and how is the amiable and charming Bartola?"

"Ichthszolckotetl!" he replied, in the Aztec language, "flourishing to a degree, and well we may be, while the dollars turn in at their present ratio. We are soon off to exhibit before the crowned heads of Europe, in which tour our governor rather calkilates to realize—but, hold! —I am betraying secrets."

Here an idea struck me suddenly

"Marvellous descendant of the Aztecs, or Tontecs, or Prince of Teck's, or whatever thou art," I cried, "say, how would you like it, if you and the charming Bartola were seated on the throne of your native Mexico?"

"Stranger," replied the offended Señor Nunez, "we may not be any extensive pumpkins in the intellectual line; but I reckon we're not quite such consummate idiots as that comes to! Scarcely!"

At this moment a frightful yell was heard across the prairie. We all stopped, paralyzed, epileptic, and rheumatic with sheer terror. I knew the sound; it was the war-cry of our dreaded enemies — a cry which proved that, though a red man, the Skull Hunter is none the less a yeller.

I knew the characters of our foes to be such
that they would have their revenge, even on
those who had never done them any injury Such
is the deadly enmity which ever exists between
the red man of the forest and the pale of civilization !

I swept the horizon with my telescope (of
course, greatly purifying it by the operation),
and discovered a young single file of Indians
behind, and an old married file of an Indian in
front ; they were all actively engaged in washing
the ugly, or, in other words, scouring the plain.
They were coming down upon us, and were so
plentiful that we endeavoured to make ourselves
scarce.

But it was too late ; they were gaining on us
every moment. Flight, resistance, resignation,
were alike unavailing. What could we do?
Nothing, but break off the chapter suddenly,
with the usual—

*　　*　　*　　*　　*

CHAPTER XI.

ANOTHER PRETTY PRAIRIE PREDICAMENT.

Such, reader, was our situation, and it is no wonder that we were quite ready to give it up, and, if necessary, to advertise for another.

In such a strait, even the most crooked way of escape would have been straightway adopted.

We held a consultation, but the symptoms were so dangerous, that it was impossible to find any remedy.

At length the whole party came to a determination to die in defence of their lives or perish in the attempt.

Ah! reader, it was a bitter moment; wormwood was nothing to it. Brigham Young thought of his four hundred and sixty-six wives, and shed a tear for each, mournfully remarking that killing him was equal to murdering four hundred and sixty-six ordinary husbands. Señor Maximo Nunez sobbed in the purest Aztec as he thought of his Bartola, and naturally considered the conduct of the Indians bar-barous and in-tola-rant to a degree. Prince Maximilian thought of the crown he had lost, and the five shillings he had in his pocket, and finally resolved to sell his life dearly, and live upon the proceeds ever afterwards.

Bill Bowie thought of the hut the Indians had burnt — which was certainly a burning shame—and the impossibility in such a scrape as this of coming up to the scratch.

Meanwhile, both the Indians and the atmosphere were becoming closer every moment.

I was the only one of the party who had no need for retrospective reflection. Why should I look backwards into futurity? I had lost all, and, in fact, rather more, and all I could do now was to look out for myself, for which purpose I found the telescope very handy.

It struck me, too, that my companions were all quite big enough—if not too big—to take care of themselves; so I sloped off down the nearest incline, unseen and unsuspected.

It is a remarkable fact that my courage is of that order which increases the further I am removed from danger; and I felt perfectly heroic as I streaked cautiously off into the forest, leaving my companions in the lurch, which was fortunately quite large enough to contain them.

Overcome as I was with fear-(lessness), I was still conscious enough to know that if I could once get out of harm's way I should be safe. It also struck me that the quicker I went, the sooner I should get away from my enemies. Such is the exalted pitch to which imminent danger quickens the perceptive faculties!

I soon found myself spinning along through a completely impenetrable forest, at a pace which the quickest express trains would shudder to contemplate. My position was still terrible. On my track were the remorseless Indians. Around me was a thick forest of pine and Harrison trees, stretching as far as the eye could reach; and right in my path a tremendous mountain gorge, overgrown with gorgeous vegetation; there were, besides, a grizzly bear and a boa-constrictor on every tree, while two jaguars and a panther lay concealed behind the rocks, ready for a spring— or summer as the case might be. All these animals were evidently thirsting for my blood in quantities varying from half a pint to nine gallons, according to their capacities.

How to get away from the Indians, leap the chasm, dodge the grizzlies, chaw up the boa-

A WIDE LEAP AND A NARROW ESCAPE.

constrictors, and elude the panthers, "that"—
as Dante appropriately remarks — " was the
question." My only means of defence consisted
of three donkey-guns and two horse-pistols.
together with a telescope, two bowie-knives, and
a tooth-pick. What might, could, would, or
should I do under such circumstances?

My life hung upon a thread—(Boar's head,
No. 40),—and the fate of romantic prairie litera-
ture trembled in the balance!

The chasm was only thirty feet across, and
there was no earthly reason why my gallant
steed should not leap it, except his inability to
do so. This, however, I determined to overcome, and so, gently urging him with repeated
blows, I breasted him at the gulf. He gave a
bound, but in the middle of the leap, when he
was half way across, he suddenly changed his
mind, and, turning round, leapt back again.

CHAPTER XII.

STILL IN DANGER.

HE conse-
quences of this
rash act may
be better de-
scribed than
imagined.

The whole of
the grizzlies,
snakes, pan-
thers, &c. leapt
upon me at
once. I could
see at a glance
that these ani-
mals had form-
ed themselves
into a Mexican Prairie Predatory and Man-
hunting Company (Unlimited), and I was destined
to become their first dividend.

Ah! how I longed to be far away! How much
sooner would I have undergone ten thousand
Parisian carnival fêtes than such a Mexican
carnival fate as this! How I wished that my
horse's trail could take me to far Horse-trailia!

But it was not to be; there was no escape;
no way of getting through, or round, or out of
the difficulty I was not at all hungry, but I
knew that I should soon make a good meal for
my enemies.

   *   *   *   *   *

Stay! there was one chance—faint as a two-
year-old photograph—but still a gleam of hope!
Stratagem—a gem, indeed, under such circumstances—alone could save me.

Concealing myself beneath my cloak, I proceeded to alter my appearance. By means of
some hair dye, blacking, &c., I quickly transformed myself into an Indian. To change my
dress, my skin, my hair, my expression, was, of
course, the work of a moment.

Thus transformed, I suddenly lifted up my
head and confronted my enemies.

"Away, varmints, or you shall be squashed!"
I thundered; "I am a SKULL HUNTER!"

The effect of this dreaded name upon the
animals was almost magical. The snakes fell

into each others' arms in strong convulsions; the bears, already grizzly, became grey all over; the panthers panted, and exhibited dangerous symptoms of heart disease; and the jaguars grew visibly thinner with anxiety.

Taking advantage of this general consternation, I whispered a few words of flattery, and warning, and command, into the ear of my noble steed, which he quickly understood! and as I undid his girths to give him greater ease, he felt both bound and unbound to leap across the chasm.

Landing safely on the other side, several packs of wolves gave chase after me, each pack, of course, containing fifty-two, and artful cards most of them were. But I evaded them, and kept on at such a headlong pace that my horse entirely left off touching the ground.

But how mistaken I was in my calculations! While exulting over the prospect of escape, I rode suddenly into the very centre of a party of Skull Hunters.

They were so sharp, that they easily penetrated my disguise, and the same remark applies to the arrows with which they overwhelmed me.

I was speedily seized and carried, with a shattered constitution and a liver damaged beyond recovery, into the presence of the ubiquitous Wanderoga.

"Away with him!" bellowed the terrific chieftain; "away with him instantly to the Tents of Torture!!!"

CHAPTER XIII.

THE TENTS OF TORTURE.

THE appearance of Indian tents is of course well known to the main readers of prairie novels, as they form some of the chief hits of Aim-hard, and one of the best p'ints of Cooper. Should any of my readers, however, be afflicted with ignorance on the subject, I am ready to give them a yard and a half of description at a minute's notice.

The tents of the Skull Hunters were disposed in an oblongular parallelogrammatical form. Each tent was supported by Poles—(though, we believe, discountenanced by Russians)—and covered with Mexican skins, Indian skins, Russ-skins, &c. The Tents of Torture were only to be approached by the most torturous windings, and thither I was carried on the points of Indian spears—about the most painful mode of convey-ance I ever ex-spear-ienced.

In the principal tent sat the captive Donna
Isabella, found at last, though lost in reflection,
and her countenance expressed that degree of
mental agony which can only be conceived by
persons listening to the tearing of calico, or the
tuning of a violin.

Beside her stood the chair, and likewise the
form, of an Indian maiden of majestic aspect.
(N.B.—In all tales of the Prairie, Indian mai-
dens are indispensable.)

Her appearance I was too agitated to notice;
but I can, of course, describe it minutely, by
that intuitive faculty possessed by all writers of
romance. Her complexion was so dark that I
didn't consider it fair at all—no more I did my
own treatment by the Indians. Her nose, and
likewise her eyes, had an-hazel appearance, and
her whole features were cast in a classic mould—
probably of plaster of Paris. Her expression
was knowing, but her dress was simple to a fault
—what fault I was at a loss to conjecture—ornamented with stripes *à la* cat-o'-nine-tails, and
stars *à la* Telescope-de-Rosse.

She wore leather moke-assins, such as are in
use among Indian ass-ass-ins in general, perfectly
bead-izened with beads of all kinds, especially
bugles, which of course gave them rather a loud

appearance. In short, her costume exactly corresponded with the fashion plates in *Le Follet des Prairies*, which, as every reader knows, is published on the 32nd of each month.

This remarkable woman looked daggers—including the sheaths—at Isabella and myself; and in her hand she held a gun, which showed that her intentions were not pacific—probably they were Atlantic.

I found that this Indian maiden was no other than Ma-ree-waw-ka, the medicine-woman of the tribe, and of course physic-ally superior to any other chieftainess. She was related to the renowned chief, Hoo-kee-waw-ka, surnamed the Humbug of the Rocky Mountains, and was likewise betrothed to the great Wanderoga.

The latter warrior, regardless alike of the dark looks of his *fiancée*, and the light in which she regarded him, shortly afterwards entered the tent. He had made his toilet, and a considerable toil-it must have been to him. He had on a fresh coat of paint, and a waistcoat of the same material, ornamented with the pattern popularly known as His Satanic Majesty's tattoo, together with several other designs in the pre-Raphaelite style. His hair had been brushed by machinery, and his manners polished with patent blacking. His language was that of one deep in love and Lindley Murray

"Fairest Isabella!" he cried, flinging himself at her feet, "long have I been paying my addresses—though the bill was not sent in,—vouchsafe, however, to say you will return my affection."

"Avaunt!" she cried, "thy bones are marrow"—

"—Less," he replied, "very much less, Señora. But why this rejectiousness and contemptuosity? I love thee with an affection that is killing me by inches—if not yards. Say thou wilt be mine, and the whole of my wealth—principally consisting of scalps and wampum belts—shall be poured at thy feet. For thee will I kill the biggest buffaloes, the cantankerest jaguars. All the rank and fashion of the neighbouring tribes shall do thee homage, and thou shalt have a box at every opera-house in the prairie."

"Never!" she replied; "ugly as thou mayst be, thou art not the complete object of my affections. Wanderoga, I can never be thine; therefore, wander, ogre, from my presence for ever!"

The proud chief sprang to his feet, mauve with rage—

"False one, I will be avenged!" he cried.

" What, ho! let her chignon be instantly ampu-
tated.   Let the operation be as painful as possible!   Hither, ye torturers!"

He quitted the tent, and the Indian maiden
came forward with an expression of ecstasy and
a dance of delight.

CHAPTER XIV

THE MEDICINE WOMAN.

AR-R-R-AH!" yelled the Indian maiden, "this then is my revenge! What! shall a daughter of the pale-faces approach the presence of an Indianess otherwise than on all-fours, and not be crucified? No, no. She must be sacrificed, and thou, too, pale-faced chief, on the altar of the great Mumbo Jumbo, whom we worship."

"And is that the 'divinity' that is to 'shape our ends?'" I asked, scornfully

"Blasphemite!" exclaimed the medicine wo-man, "dare to repeat those words and thou shalt be ground to pieces in a Stuart Mill."

At this moment the torturers rushed in, headed by the terrible chief, Hoo-kee-waw-ka, a man who seemed to breathe, as it were, an atmosphere of blood, and whose deeds of murder were brought out in weekly numbers.

O horror! the torturers bring the fatal scissors, the murderous comb!

They are about to amputate the chignon of the guileless Isabella.   And I—I was to witness the frightful sacrifice!!   The excruciating agony of the thought was too horrible to endure.   I started up with a shriek of despair, and strove to shut out the murderous scene with my hands; and then, faint with anguish and excitement, sank back into the arms of my captors.

*   *   *   *   *

A vision as of five million gregarines floated across my bewildered brain, until, with a groan, I became insensible.

*   *   *   *   *

When I recovered, all was over.   The sacrifice had been made, the victim immolated, and the

INDIAN PURGATORY OR HAIR-DESTROYER.

medicine woman, with a howl of triumph, held aloft the persecuted and blighted chignon.

And to add even to these horrors, Donna Isabella was hung up to the side of the tent by her remaining tresses, each particular hair made to stand on end, and tied carefully around the rafters that supported the roof.

The fearful chief, Hoo-kee-waw-ka, came forward and seized me.

"Greyhound of a wan complexion!" he thundered—(N.B. This was an elegant variation of "Dog of a pale-face")—"thine hour is come. At least," he added, referring to his watch, "it only wants about two minutes. Our chiefs have sworn you shall die a thousand deaths, but I am merciful, and will limit them to five hundred."

"Spare me, great chief," I murmured.

"Never!" he answered. "Though I consider myself 'a few,' I am not one to spare. Thou shalt suffer the slowest tortures. Fifty years' indescribable agony will teach you what it is to dare to exist, when the Skull Hunters had rather you wouldn't. Torturers, to your work!"

Which they did. Readers, allow me to ask you, for about the thousandth time I have put the question, What was I to do? also, Where was Bill Bowie? What had become of the Arch-

Duke? Who had chawed up the Aztec? How was the Prophet getting on? What will you take to drink? &c.

Yes, what was I to do? Death stared me in the face in the rudest possible manner, and my thread of life had waxed tight indeed!

*   *   *   *   *

Poor Isabella had a large placard tied round her neck, bearing the following mystic inscription, " 350TH NIGHT OF BLACK-EYED SUSAN!"

At this the Indians intended to fire.

The torturers next tortured me with torches, applied to my whiskers and other vital parts.

Then they fastened me to the wall with tin-tacks, painted the likeness of Count Von Bis-marck on my unprotected breast, and commenced blazing away at it.

Heavens! what a fate! What would be the end of it? Would it justify the means?

CHAPTER XV

THE INDIAN FEAST.

THE fact is, my hour really *had* come at last—
every man, according to the testimony of the
most distinguished novelists, has his hour, and
though it is frequently a long time coming, it
is sure to come at last—in this respect differ-
ing greatly from to-morrow, or policemen when
wanted.

Ah me! was I to fall a victim to the horrible
custom of skull-hunting? Yes, it must be so;
my unlucky pate and skull were to suffer, and
from this dreadful doom nothing could ex-skull-
pate me!

But first the Indians, inspired by bitter ale,
and still more bitter hatred, commenced firing
away at me with cross-bows and disagreeable
arrows, poisoned and exorbitantly charged with
gunpowder at the tip!

Seeing these projectiles coming, I steeled myself and hardened my heart against them—the
only way to deaden their effect.

Donna Isabella and myself were shot at simultaneously and alternately, and we reciprocally felt for each other to that degree, that I only experienced pain from the wounds she received, and *vice versá*, consequently I hoped she wouldn't get hurt, though I was too heroic to care about my own injuries.

Wanderoga, Hoo-kee-waw-ka, and the Medicine woman directed the aim of the men, who were making a kind of Newington Butts of us. Every time an arrow reached me, the Indians burst into a flood of laughter, and the tent resounded with a Sir Robert—or, rather, General Peel. Every man held his sides, and well he might, as the laugh was entirely on his side. Their mirth was completely at my expense, which was very mean on their part, for though I don't mind standing a Morning Smile, I can't endure a midnight laugh.

When they had shot until they all dropped from exhaustion, the Indians divided, and went into Supply—of provisions—in a most parliamentary manner. They held a feast of deer-meat, which is about the cheapest meat to be obtained on the prairies, and put themselves outside an amount of liquor which only the pen of a Cruikshank can adequately describe.

The mirth and wassail increased, and jestivity
and festification became the order of the day
(which was not admitted after seven).

Then they sang, "We are na fou," "Jolly
Nose," and many more of Mendelssohn's beautiful "Songs without words" or music. Some
of them composed extempore melodies, almost
equal in quality to those gorgeous effusions
heard nightly at the London music halls; and
others danced *pas seuls*, and delivered speeches,
in a manner that would have done credit to the
Pas-seuls' Delivery Company.

Many of them drank until their utterance was
so thick you could have cut it with a knife—
indeed, the Indians did cut it shortly afterwards,
leaving Donna Isabella and myself alone at last,
in solitude and excruciation.

I had about five hundred wounds, and Isabella
about two hundred and fifty, so that, according
to our feelings of mutual sympathy, she had
rather the worst of it.

But I determined on revenge, even if it took
three volumes to describe it.

CHAPTER XVI.

THE WOLF WITH NIGHTLY PROWL.

*   *   *

OLITUDE and gloom were now added to the horrors of our situation.

*   *   *

We were alone. Night had fallen (hurting itself very much). The darkness was the only thing visible, and that could be only discerned by the aid of a powerful telescope.

*   *   *   *   *

Hark! hush!! silence!!! listen!!!! breathlessly, speechlessly, unswervingly!!!!! What
cry is that? What are those terriferocious
sounds that curdle the blood, and turn the
milky whey into deadly ice?

It are wolves!

Yes, reader, wolves. They can scent us out
from the distance with all the skill of Rimmel
himself.

*   *   *   *   *

Nearer come the horrid sounds!

*   *   *   *   *

The sentinel wolf reaches the door of the
tent. He stops for about two seconds to kill
and eat the Indian sentry outside, and then
makes his-entry inside.

The monster sees us with a grin of delight,
and stands on his head in glee.

Our fate was sealed. Should we be justified
in breaking it open? I thought of General
Wolfe—in fact, my mind was entirely filled with
wolves, as I reflected that their bodies would
soon be filled with me.

Another wolf looked into the door of the tent,
and then it-ent-ered. Others followed. Their
name (according to the Directory) was Legion.

A thousand wolfish eyes glared at us so brilliantly that the tent was as light as day, if not lighter.

The first thing they did was to gnaw out the fastenings that fixed us to the wall, in a gnawful manner.

I had about five hundred arrows in me. The true instincts of a Yankee inspired me with a magnificent scheme to be revenged on my enemies.

I would extract the arrows, and sell them at a large profit! ! !

I tore them out in handfuls as I leapt from the wall, and waved them around my head!

The wolves were skeered. I proceeded to rescue Isabella.

" Señor victorious! " she cried, as she sprang joyfully into my arms.

" Happy and glorious! " I replied gleefully.

" Long to rain over us! " she said, alluding to the weather.

" God save the queen—of my affections! " I shouted, as, clasping her to my breast, I cleared at a bound the three hundred wolves, and plunged into the boundless prairie.

PICTURESQUE EFFECT—A WATERFALL BY MOONLIGHT.

CHAPTER XVII.

THE SERENADE.

SCARCELY half a quarter of a second was lost in this, my five hundred and fifty-fifth prairie escape. Long before the wolves could cry "Jack Robinson," or indeed make any e-jackulation whatever, I had reached the saddle of my beloved steed, while Donna had comfortably settled herself on the tail of the animal. But remembering that two horses could, of course, go quicker than one, I lassoed another steed, which Isabella mounted, and tied the two bridles together, thus increasing our pace twofold.

The speed we went at was a caution to most things. Many a flash of lightning tried to overtake us, but perished in the attempt; many a thunderbolt missed us by half a mile; and the most powerful telescope would have been worn out in any attempt to follow our movements.

The wolves were after us as quick as winking;

but they found it no use, so they all died of rage
and disappointment; and the remainder turned
to and mutually devoured each other to satisfy
their hungry and angry cravings.

Still we went on, skimming the surface of the
ground, which produced a rich and delightful
cream.

At length, after a ride over an awful extent
of country, we all fell down exhausted at the
door of an *hacienda*, at the further end of the
perilous prairie.

The *pulquero*, or landlord of the *hacienda*,
benevolently agreed to take us in at the small
figure of forty-five dollars. Considering how
we had knocked him up, it was perhaps rather
unfair to beat him down; but I told him not to
take on at the idea of taking off a few dollars,
He at length consented; and while Donna
Isabella disappeared from my sight, I reposed
myself to slumber in a small chamber, containing not more than twenty-five travellers,
and about two thousand musquitoes, fleas, &c.

I slept the sleep of the sleepy, and dreamed
that I dwelt in marble halls, which, being near
the sea-girt shore, gave me a capital view of
the vessels and surfs by my side, until I awoke
suddenly. The atmosphere was at about one

hundred and fifty in the dark; the mosquitoes were amazing lively, and the whole of my companions were performing a variety of deep bass concertos on their nasal organs. Under these circumstances, I thought I would rise on this occasion; so I rose, attired myself in the most gorgeous Mexican costume I could find without a light, and borrowing a guitar from a sleeping cavalier, whose silence gave consent, I smashed three panes of glass, and leapt lightly into the garden.

Ah, reader! it was a lovely spot; the verdant big-nonia (which is, of course, but little known here) waved its branches on every side; while the silvery beet-root, and the delightful magnum bonum, sobbed in harmony with the tuneful silence.

The weather, too, had changed considerably; the wind had long been in the East, but had now returned with a thorough knowledge of Oriental manners and customs; the moon was full almost to bursting; the stars were out, but willing to accept provincial engagements; and the filmy clouds were enough to fill-my heart with pleasurable emotions.

The effect of all this was, that I determined to serenade Donna Isabella. So I struck the

light guitar, turned up my eyes till only the
pupil was visible, took a deep fill of poetical
inspiration, and commencing at O sharp, plunged
into the following beautiful melody :—

SERENADE.

Oh, gorgeous land of Mexico,
   Where fruits and pumpkins blossom,
Where dwell the snake and buffalo,
   The jaguar and the 'possum;
All things thou hast of scrumptiousness
   To fascinate a fellah,
But all are licked to fits, I guess,
   By lovely Isabella!
Her eyes are like the Mountain Dhu,
   Her nose is much the same ;
Her hair (chignon included) outshines in brilliant hue
   Petroleum's ambient flame.
My heart is bursting with delight,
   To gaze on thee once more,
So come thou forth, my lady bright,
   And give me one *encore !*

O Saccharissima ! what is this assortment of
fluid that descends upon my classical but devoted
head? Is it Niagara, or a shower of rain, or
(oh, horrific thought!) can it be the contents of
the water-jug?

   *   *   *   *   *

The idea was madness; so seeing nothing
else to do, I fell upon the grass in a strong
hydrophobic fit of insensibility.

   *   *   *   *   *

How long I lay in this condition I know not (as I didn't have my watch with me), but when I arose, the sun was making a terrific shine in the firmament, and the morning lark was trying to make up for the evening's spree by a variety of operatic selections.

I arose, but found, to my sorrow, that my chivalric Mexican suit was entirely spoilt, heavy wet had been the ruin of it, and made it cling to me so, that I gave up all thoughts of returning it to the owner, for I was obliged to stick to it myself. As to the guitar, it was so saturated, that from that time forth nothing could be played on it but Handel's Water Music!

* * * * *

CHAPTER XVIII.

THE LOVE DECLARATION.

ENTERED. She was re-clining on a *barège* divan, attired in a mantilla of *tulle illusion*, and her appearance was so delectious, that I can only speak of it in super-lative terms. She was the most per-fectest of her sex! I placed a cambric hand-kerchief on the floor, knelt on it carefully, and looked up at her with no end of expression.

"Enchantingest one!" I faltered; "thou whose eyes outglisten the blossoms of the dulcet cabbage, and whose flowing locks surpass those of Chubb and Bramah, listen to the words of true affection. I love thee to that extent, that in thy presence my heart stops beating, and my pulse rises to two hundred in the shade. My affection for thee out-tops that of the ring-tailed roarer or the lively golopossumus. Say, dearest one, what is thy respected father's income?"

"Five thousand pistoles," she replied.

"Then you are indeed mine own!" I cried, in the most gushing rapture; "those pistoles will shuit me exactly, and, possessing them, thy father must always be a great gun, and well loaded with wealth. Say, can you love me then as now, or at any other time that will suit your own convenience?"

The adorable one concealed her emotions behind a scent-bottle, as she replied, "I'll do my utmost possible!"

"Then I will leave you in hope," I cried, "and call in a day or two for your ultimatum. Dearest Isabella, I am still surrounded by pressing dangers, and should I fall, I have the consolation of knowing you will pick me up!!!"

My eyes swam in tears; but the eyes of Lady

Isabella — which had evidently not learned swimming—were completely drowned in tears, all the lifeboats proving entirely useless.

So, while her eyes thus went down to the floor, I went down the stairs, with the intention of drowning my own emotions in a glass of something short.

I went into the bar of the *hacienda*, which was full of persons of all kinds, and there, among them, consuming a private smile, with all the coolness imaginable, was my old friend Bill Bowie.

"Is this the Captin that I see before me?" he cried in amazement.

"Bill Bowie, or I do forget myself!" I exclaimed.

"Captin," said the trapper, "I'm all-fired glad to see you. Let us fraternally embrace."

And we fraternally embroce.

"Captin," said Bill, "what's your especial depravity in the liquor trade? Name your destroyer, and we'll both put ourselves outside a grown-up dose!"

I told him; and Bill, immediately turning to the bar-tender, said, "Squire, fix us two cocktails of gin and gunpowder, real smart."

"And now, Bill," I said, "tell me how you

got over the difficulties by which you were surrounded?"

" We didn't get over 'em, they got over us," he said. " As soon as we saw the Injines coming, we lay down between their lines, and they passed over us as neat as a whistle, for they were going at such a goll-fired speed that they couldn't stop under three miles. By the time they come to turn back, we'd all picked ourselves up considerable spray, and made tracks. We parted, and all went separate ways. I steered in this direction, and here I am to a slight extent!"

While Bill was exploring the depths of his tumbler, I related to him all my own adventures, and we continued drinking till we both had mutually to support each other.

Suddenly a terrific cry arose in the *hacienda,* of " The Skull Hunters!" and sure enough a battalion of those prairie-fiends rushed in upon us.

CHAPTER XIX.

THE CONFLICT IN THE HACIENDA.

In they rushed, with a series of wild and tame yells, every one armed with an Armstrong, or, at least, a strong arm. They appeared the most bloodthirsty ruffians that ever drew the breath of life, or the trigger of death; their ferocity out-wolved the prairie wolf, and licked every bear—including cubs—into the neatest of fits.

What could we do? We were but twenty weak, and the Indians were five hundred strong!

For my own part, I stood firm as an aspen; and yet my heart sank until it reached the pit of my stomach, giving me the indigestion powerful bad. I felt as if I could sink through the earth and come out at the antipodes, but I didn't.

The better part of valour prompted me to look out for myself. Why should I stay and be killed, while there was any chance of getting away? It would be the act of an insaniac!

A SLIGHT DISAGREEMENT WITH THE SKULL HUNTERS.

But it was too late. All hope of escape was over. Every one of the doors, windows, chimneys, key-holes, &c., had been carefully stopped up with corks, patent vent-pegs, &c., and millions of Indians surrounded the *hacienda* on all sides.

At this terrible juncture, I asked Bill what he intended to do.

"Stay here and lick 'em to fine sawdust," was his valorous reply. "What! air I a Yank for nuthin'? Do I belong to a nation that can wollop the world before breakfast, and shall I levant from an all-fired cuss of an Injin? Never! Come on, ye skunks! and blowed for ever be the first that funks!"

And they did come on with a vengeance, headed by the frightful Wanderoga and the terrific Hoo-kee-waw-ka.

"Chaw 'em up, the blow-fired varmints of pale-faces!" bellowed these chiefs in unison. "Skull 'em, scalp 'em, skin 'em, grind 'em to salt, pepper their livers, and turn off their gas-tric juices at the main!"

The Indians yelled as one man in reply to these horrible orders.

The fight was fearful—so fearful that I cannot find words to describe it, though I have bought five dictionaries for the purpose.

Standing behind the bar of the *hacienda*, I served out several doses of something very strong to the Indians. None can say that I didn't serve them right, or omitted to give them the best my barrels contained.

The battle increased in fierceness. The way the Indians skulled, scalped, fought, bit, tore, scratched, stabbed, fired, and blazed away, was enough to frighten the stripes off a zebra. Blood, smoke, fire, fury, yells, groans, execrations, wounded Yanks, chawed-up Indians, and general confusion, prevailed considerably.

I thought of Isabella. I rushed upstairs. Gone! gone! how, when, where, was a mystery. I clenched my moustache and ground my eyelids in anguish, as I rushed back to the scene of conflict.

We fought like steam-engines, but in vain. The Skull Hunters, by their superior numbers, got the victory. When it was first given out that our leader had given in, we felt that we were no longer ungone 'coons.

Yes, the Redskins were victorious. They had taken twenty skulls and no end of scalps, but had themselves suffered slightly   Many of our party were rather killed, but, fortunately, not much.

A universal chawedupness prevailed everywhere.

As to the house, it was knocked completely into a cocked hat, which the triumphant chief placed on his head as a trophy of victory   It fitted him beautifully.

CHAPTER XX.

THE LAST STRUGGLE.

E fled. Some of us at the top of our speed, and others at the bottom ; the Indians pursued.

We had an object in acting thus. I had ascertained, by looking at my prairie almanack, that there was to be an eruption of Mount Ictolteclocatapetl at seven o'clock that morning, and thought that if we could lead the Indians on to it at that time (getting clear off ourselves on the other side), our enemies would be blown up beyond all possibility of answering back.

So we made tracks for the volcano. But fate and a precipice forbade, and there we were, on the brink of a frightful abyss, with thousands of Indians behind us. Moreover, there were more over the other side of the small lake, armed with spears (a case of Spiers and Pond), and we had no way of crossing the black well-like chasm (a case of Crosse and Blackwell), so that we were again in a fix.

    *   *   *   *   *

I fled in a circumvolvular direction, leaving my comrades on the brink of the precipice. Wanderoga and a full Indian file were after me full chisel.

I was chased into a small claim in the forest, where Wanderoga overtook me. I was in his power. The chief knew it, and sharpened his scalping-knife accordingly

"Cabbage-livered skunk!" he bellowed, his eyes flashing with fire and life assurance, "thine hour of spiflication hath come. Prepare for thine death."

He grasped my throat, and having lit his wind-pipe with a sculling match, raised aloft his murderous knife.

"Unthirsty and blood-sparing wretch!" I thundered, "I command you to hold hard. Think you that I have not discovered your vile secret—thou art JUAREZ, the MEXICAN CHIEF!!!"

Appalling was the effect of these words on the Indian. He recoiled, his eyes started several inches out of his head, both the pupils and teachers becoming invisible. His giant form dilated, grew taller, broader, fuller, rose higher and higher, expanded and distended to leviathan dimensions. His countenance was swollen to suffocation by the livid fury that consumed him.

The very ground around him grew hot—and hotter, and hotter—

   *   *   *   *   *

Still the horrible figure of the Indian becoming larger and larger, and—oh, heavens!—filling up the entire landscape, shutting out all other objects, and making me think I am mad!

   *   *   *   *   *

Oh, mercy! how long will this continue?

   *   *   *   *   *

I close my eyes in cold horror. Then a burst, a report, an explosion like twenty thousand minute-guns, and I look up again, and see

A TERRIFIC EXPLOSION ON THE PART OF WANDEROGA.

nothing of Wanderoga but a wreath of sulphurous smoke.

* * * * *

The terrific chief had died of spontaneous combustion ! ! !

* * * * *

"There is one miscreant less in the world," cried Bill Bowie. (Which there was.)

* * * * *

But our party were getting the worst of it.

Stay, there is help at hand !

What is that welcome body of armed men in the distance coming to our rescue ?

O joy ! it is a band of Mexican banderillas !— O joyer ! it is led by Don Bartolomeo, Isabella's father !—O joyest ! there is Isabella herself, clinging to him as the vine-tendril clings to its parent oak ! They charge in among the disordered Indians and put them to the rout. A fight more desperate than any commences.

A fight for life ! A scene so terrific that I have never in my life beheld a terrificker !

* * * * *

All is over ! The rest of the Skull Hunters have followed their chief's example to a man— and a woman—the two latter being the Chief

Hoo-kee-waw-ka, and his relative, the medicine woman.

The remainder of the Skull Hunters were either killed, or died such frightful colours that we were obliged to put them out of their misery

Thus perished the mocassined scourges of the prairie.

"Now," I cried, to the two surviving prisoners, "as you two are the only ones left, you must both die, as a warning to the rest!"

The Chief Hoo-kee-waw-ka fell at my feet. "I am no Skull Hunter," he cried abjectedly; "hear, see, and believe."

He flung off his war-paint, wampum, toma-hawk, and mocassins, and appeared with a white complexion and a genteel suit of evening black.

"Can I believe my eyes?" I exclaimed, "STEPHENS, the Fenian Head-Centre!"

"Begorra, and it's myself, thrue enough," he cried. "But oh, yer honour's glory, have a thrifling taste of mercy on me. Release me and give me a thousand dollars, and it's me own self as will skedaddle to the south of France, and not trouble you nor ould Ireland again, at all at all!"

"Go," I cried, "this instant, and never come back again under pain of transfixiation!"

And he did.

"As for you," I cried, turning to Ma-ree-waw-ka, the medicine woman, "you shall be released on conditions. Will you promise never to give anatomical lectures, nor have shindies with medical students, and to abjure the Bloomer costume for ever?"

"I renounce them all!" she replied, in earnest but agonized accents.

"Then you are indeed mine!" shouted Bill Bowie, who appeared to have just thought of it.

At that moment, the Don's party approached. The scene was awfully affecting, but the scene-shifters soon afterwards removed it to make room for the grand closing *tableau*.

CHAPTER XXI.

LAST SCENE OF ALL.

ALL my dangers were over, and my foes chawed-up with that ease only attained in prairie romances.

It was time, therefore, for the end of this history to begin.

The scene was the front parlour of the posado, the ancestral residence of Don Bartolomeo de Fandango.

Don Bartolomeo was of a very noble family He was a hidalgo—one of the highest of dalgoes —and his blood was so blue that you could have painted a sky with it easily. He traced his descent (by means of tracing paper), direct from the Moors, Castilians, Iberians, Normans, Goths, Vandals, Visigoths, Ostrogoths, Abencerrages, Mesopotamians, Patagonians, Medes, Persians, &c.

Again was Isabella reclining on a muslin couch, looking the picture of loveliness (in frame

THE CAPTAIN PRESENTS HIMSELF FOR ACCEPTANCE AND IS DULY HONOURED.

complete, five dollars). Again I knelt before her in a highly picturesque manner.

"Dearest Isabella," I cried, "we have together passed through more dangers than anybody will ever believe. Come, let us be happy together; say, will you return my love cent. per cent?"

The adorable one blushed in a manner that showed great experience, and replied, "About eighty-seven and a half."

"Then I am satisfied," I replied, "though the interest is rather below par."

"As to pa," she returned, "interest is never below him. See, here he comes." The Don entered; I threw myself before him, and addressed him in this strain,—

"Highly aristocratic and important bloke, hear my request. *Donnez-moi*, Don, *cette jeune donna :* were you the donor of this gift, I'd-honour you for ever. Give me but the hand,"—

"'Tis hard to give the hand," he remarked.

"True," I replied, "but it is ardour for me to speak thus."

"Young man," said the Don, "let me first ask you a few important questions: are you noble?"

"Noble, I should think I was," I replied;

"my ancestors came over to America with William the Conqueror, and I am nephew to the great Duke Humphrey, whom I dined with at his estate, the Balmy Side, only a week ago."

"What is your income?" asked the Don.

"Two hundred dollars per edition," I cried romantically. "I have likewise a commission as Captain in the Rapahannock Fisticuffers, besides Stars of the Order of St. Golly, St. Gum, St. Jingo, &c."

"Then, Señor," replied the Don, "you'll do. Isabella, though it's hard to give the hand where the heart can never be without a total upset of the human anatomy, still, remembering that there is a flower that bloometh, I think I am justified in making this original observation—Ber-less you, my che-hildering!"

He spread his hands over our heads and then resumed—"And if our kyind friends in front—but no matter—as I said before, ber-less you—be happy!"

And not liking to disobey him, we have been happy ever since.

*　　*　　*　　*　　*

Reader, you would not recognize the Squatter's hut, especially if you had never seen it before.

It is now a noble mansion, for Bill Bowie has speculated in petroleum and shoddy, become a Member of Congress, and amassed a considerable pittance. Neither would you recognize in Mrs. Bowie the fierce Ma-ree-waw-ka, who has now abandoned the healing art, except theoretically. She still, however, writes treatises on the subject, and has achieved much fame by her last work on "Compound Deglutition of the Epidermis."

I have produced another Prairie Novel, and a book on Mexicology and United State-istics. I was also for some time editor of the *Small Times* (which lasted a very small time indeed), the *Tiny Telegraph*, the *Infinitesimal Review*, &c., &c.

With regard to the paper entrusted to me by the unfortunate Archduke, I sent it to Andrew Johnson, who, as every one knows, is now Grand Llama of Mexico, and Tycoon of the United States.

Reader, we must now part. I have nothing more to say, and I shall therefore not be long saying it. Glorious land of Montezuma! mighty realm of Anahuac, adieu! The bald-headed eagle, soaring on all-fired wings of unmitigated liberty, looks down on thy boundless locations in general, and mine in particular; but no longer does it look down on the tents of that bloodthirsty tribe, from which my praiseworthy efforts have cleared the Prairie—the dreaded SKULL HUNTERS.

THE END.

Woodfall and Kinder, Printers, Milford Lane, Strand, London, W.C.

www.ingramcontent.com/pod-product-compliance
Lightning Source LLC
Chambersburg PA
CBHW020757020726
47495CB00008B/2479